To Trevor
and the magic of childhood

My Book

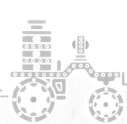

THIS IS A BORZOI BOOK PUBLISHED BY ALFRED A. KNOPF, INC.

Copyright © 1985 by Lynn Hollyn Associates, Incorporated
All rights reserved under International and Pan-American Copyright Conventions.
Published in the United States by Alfred A. Knopf, Inc., New York,
and simultaneously in Canada by Random House of Canada Limited, Toronto.
Distributed by Random House, Inc., New York.
Manufactured in the United States of America.   1 2 3 4 5 6 7 8 9 0

Library of Congress Cataloging in Publication Data
Hollyn, Lynn. Lynn Hollyn's Christmas toyland.
Summary: After the children fall asleep on Christmas Eve, their toys travel
to the land of Christmas Wood where they have a wonderful feast with the fairies.
1. Children's stories, American. [1. Christmas—Fiction. 2. Toys—Fiction]
I. Anzalone, Lori, ill. II. Title. III. Title: Christmas toyland.
PZ7.H7315Ly 1985 [E] 85-5212
ISBN 0-394-87631-8   ISBN 0-394-97631-2 (lib. bdg.)

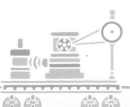

LYNN HOLLYN'S
CHRISTMAS
TOYLAND

PAINTINGS·LORI ANZALONE

ALFRED A. KNOPF
NEW YORK

s evening came to the village of Skona the last shoppers were hurrying home through the gently falling snow. Under their arms were gaily wrapped parcels and in their hearts a whisper of something wonderful about to happen. For it was Christmas Eve.

Inside the home of the Lind family, Mama and Papa were lighting the candles and trimming the tree. Soon the parlor would be ready for the arrival of Santa. Upstairs in the nursery the children were preparing for bed.

Kristina was saying good night to her beloved dolls. Their porcelain faces were scrubbed clean, their pinafores crisply starched, and their lace trimmings lovingly mended where they had begun to fray. The dolls looked their finest for tomorrow's festivities.

Johann was inspecting his squadron of wooden soldiers. Their battle scars had been repaired with fresh coats of paint, and the brass buttons on their waistcoats had been polished. Now they stood at attention awaiting his command.

The cuddly bears and floppy rabbits sat quietly in their corner of the nursery. Kristina and Johann had given them new satin bows, and their glass eyes shone with excitement.

At last Kristina and Johann were tucked into their beds, and after a very long time of whispering and tossing and turning, they closed their eyes and went to sleep. And just in the nick of time . . .

for when the clock chimed
midnight, the toys sprang to
life! The dolls in their satin
best curtsied to the soldiers.
The soldiers in full regalia
politely bowed to the dolls.
Then, two by two, they
began to promenade.

The stuffed bears waddled forward and the
bunnies hippity-hopped across the floor. Even
the dappled rocking horse joined the parade.
Silently the toys crept onto the window seat
and pulled open the window. Outside, lacy
snowflakes beckoned.

Each toy slipped into the night. The dancing snowflakes carried them far from the nursery and deep into the land of Christmas Wood.

Little fairies with wings
spun of sugar welcomed the
toys to Christmas Wood.
Merry elves perched on the
branches, strumming golden
harps and playing silver flutes.

As the music softly filled the glade, the soldiers and the dolls, the bears and the bunnies, joined hands and waltzed in unison. Even the winter flowers began to nod their heads.

When the music faded,
the fairies led the toys to
a banquet table laden with
cinnamon strudel and pots
of hot chocolate, marzipan
cookies and whipped cream
cakes, peppermint ice cream
with raspberry sauce, ginger-
bread boys with raisin buttons,
and every kind of delicious
treat you can imagine.

Throughout the night the toys danced and feasted. Then, just before dawn, Santa's sleigh bells were heard tinkling in the sky. The toys quickly hugged each other good night. Their Christmas Ball had ended, and it had indeed been a merry one.

Only you know their secret, for Kristina and
Johann would never guess why their toys'
cheeks were rosier and their tummies rounder.

ABOUT THIS BOOK

Every Christmas Eve as a child Lynn Hollyn heard this story from her mother. And so the story was passed from generation to generation in the real Lind family in Skona, Sweden.

Lynn Hollyn, who was named after her distant cousin Jenny Lind, the famous singer, thinks of this tale as a Swedish *Nutcracker,* though simpler and more appropriate for very young children. Now she brings the magic of this story to all children in a beautifully designed book with illustrations and borders reminiscent of nineteenth-century Sweden.